A Plane Goes

Ka-ZOOM!

Jonathan London
illustrated by **Denis Roche**

Christy Ottaviano Books
Henry Holt and Company ◆ New York

This book belongs to:

_____

Henry Holt and Company, LLC
Publishers since 1866
175 Fifth Avenue
New York, New York 10010
www.HenryHoltKids.com

Library of Congress Cataloging-in-Publication Data
London, Jonathan.
A plane goes ka-zoom! / by Jonathan London ; illustrated by Denis Roche. — 1st ed.
p.   cm.
"Christy Ottaviano Books."
Summary: Easy-to-read, rhyming text describes
the sounds of, and uses for, different kinds of airplanes.
ISBN 978-0-8050-8970-7
[1. Stories in rhyme. 2. Airplanes—Fiction.] I. Roche, Denis (Denis M.), ill. II. Title.
PZ8.3.L8433Pl 2010   [E]—dc22   200902925

First Edition—2010 / Designed by Véronique Lefèvre Sweet
The artist used gouache on paper to create the illustrations for this book.
Printed in June 2010 in China by Macmillan Production (Asia) Ltd, Kwun Tong,
Kowloon, Hong Kong, on acid-free paper. ∞
Supplier Code: 10

1 3 5 7 9 10 8 6 4 2

For Diego, David, and plane lovers, young and old
—J. L.

For Graham and Ronan, with love
—D. R.

A plane could fly fast.

A plane could fly slow.

A plane could fly high . . .

. . . or very, very low.

A plane could be silver.
A plane could be blue.

A plane could have one propeller,
or a plane could have two.

A plane goes clankety-clank.
A plane goes va-ROOM!

A plane goes zippety-zooma.
A plane goes ka-ZOOM!

A plane carries people.

A plane carries pets.

A plane carries trucks.

And a plane carries jets.

A plane's flaps slide.

A plane's engines ROAR!

A plane's lights twinkle.

A plane's wings soar.

Planes land on water.

Planes land on snow.

Planes land on runways . . .

. . . and planes come and go.

and follow the sun.

Jonathan London is the author of *A Train Goes Clickety-Clack, A Truck Goes Rattley-Bumpa*, and more than eighty books for young readers, including *Wiggle Waggle*, and the ever-popular Froggy books. He lives with his family in Graton, California.

Denis Roche is a former schoolteacher and the illustrator of *A Train Goes Clickety-Clack* and *A Truck Goes Rattley-Bumpa*. She has written and illustrated many books for young readers, including *The Best Class Picture Ever!* and *Little Pig Is Capable*. She lives with her family in Providence, Rhode Island.